Praise for Storyshares

"One of the brightest innovators and game-changers in the education industry."
— Forbes

"Your success in applying research-validated practices to promote literacy serves as a valuable model for other organizations seeking to create evidence-based literacy programs." — Library of Congress

"We need powerful social and educational innovation, and Storyshares is breaking new ground. The organization addresses critical problems facing our students and teachers. I am excited about the strategies it brings to the collective work of making sure every student has an equal chance in life."
— Teach For America

"It's the perfect idea. There's really nothing like this. I mean, wow, this will be a wonderful experience for young people." — Andrea Davis Pinkney, Executive Director, Scholastic

"Reading for meaning opens opportunities for a lifetime of learning. Providing emerging readers with engaging texts that are designed to offer both challenges and support for each individual will improve their lives for years to come. Storyshares is a wonderful start." — David Rose, Co-founder of CAST & UDL

Against All Odds

Storyshares presents

ISBN 9798885976817

Storyshares
Storyshares, LLC
24 N. Bryn Mawr Avenue #340
Bryn Mawr, PA 19010-3304
www.storyshares.org

Inspiring reading with a new kind of book.

The Bottle of Milk copyright 2024 João Cerqueira
Interest Level: Post High School   **Grade Level Equivalent:** 7.4

Tuk-Tuk copyright 2024 Hagai Perets
Interest Level: Post High School   **Grade Level Equivalent:** 4.5

988 copyright 2024 Phoebe Angaye
Interest Level: High School   **Grade Level Equivalent:** 3.1

Book design by Saskia Globig

Against All Odds

Stories of Hope in Adulthood

Storyshares

Contents

The Bottle of Milk   11
Jcão Cerqueira

Tuk-Tuk   49
Hagai Perets

988   65
Phoebe Angaye

About the Authors   78

The Bottle of Milk

João Cerqueira

1

Ukraine 1978

Maria had been in the line for food at the grocery store since dawn. She had been up at five and dragged her legs up the steep streets of Kiev to the shop. The store didn't open until 8:30.

She was wearing a gray jacket, a white sweater, a red cap, and the only pair of boots she owned.

The sun was beginning to come up. The yellow light of the few streetlamps that worked would soon go out.

The city would thaw around noon. But this early, men and women were rushing to factories and government offices. The transportation system of trains, buses, and a few private cars was waking up.

When Maria arrived, there were ninety-six people in front of her.

They all had angry faces. They were all shivering with cold. Their breath steamed from their nostrils.

None of them even acknowledged people who joined the line.

2

She took her place without acknowledging anyone either. She had to treat the others as enemies. As if they wanted to rob her of the bread and milk she needed to feed Lia, her thirteen-year-old daughter.

The line of hungry people was waiting their turn to be fed by the Communist Party in charge of the town.

They ignored the desire to break into the store.

They pretended they didn't want to steal the food ration cards from the nearest person. Those ration cards told the people at the store how much food you were allowed.

More ration cards meant more food.

But the fear of a labor camp—a prison where you worked until you collapsed... or died—made them stay in line peacefully.

Until she heard shouts.

3

"Thief, you stole my ration cards," an older woman yelled.

"Get off me, you loony," shouted a younger woman.

The younger woman was tall and pretty. The other woman was short, thick, and had a lumpy-looking face.

Both were glaring at each other, snarling like angry wolves. Maria thought the first woman was a student or a secretary. The second looked like a factory worker or cleaner.

Maria had seen this happen many times. All women, all ages, all walks of life. Always angry.

Sometimes the theft was real.

Sometimes it was just a way to take someone else's food. An accusation was often enough.

4

The younger woman pulled on the older one's hair. The older woman grabbed the younger by the throat and started to choke her. They yelled and pulled and fought.

Their two bodies looked like one enraged animal. Their struggles broke up the grocery line.

They lost their balance and fell to the ground, wrestling in the snow.

The older woman managed to get her right arm free. She curved her hand like the claw of a hawk and ripped at the other woman's face.

Bloody streaks opened up from her cheekbone to her chin.

The younger woman screamed. She sounded like a wounded animal.

Blood poured from her wounds, dripping onto the snow and her clothes.

The older woman let out a roar, stood up, snatched the young woman's shopping bag, and ran off.

5

The younger woman stayed shaking on the ground. She was bleeding. She would be scarred.

No one helped her.

A police car arrived, and two officers got out. They grabbed her, forced her into the vehicle, and took her away.

Most people pretended they weren't looking. Some actually didn't look.

No one raised their eyes.

Red stains on white snow were all that was left of the incident.

THE BOTTLE OF MILK

6

Not long afterwards, a woman called Ruth joined the line. She lived on the same street as Maria.

Although they were not friends, they knew one another. They usually greeted one another when they met in public places.

But there, in that situation, where the instinct for survival was most important, neither acknowledged the other.

Ruth stood just a few feet behind Maria and put her empty bag on the pavement.

THE BOTTLE OF MILK

7

At last, an hour later, it was Maria's turn to be served.

The grocery was dark. It smelled of flour and soap.

Instead of a door, there was a lobby with a greasy floor and a cracked marble counter. Two assistants in gray uniforms stood behind the counter.

They didn't want to be there. Maria could tell by their faces.

They inspected the ration cards and handed over the right items of food.

With her head held low, Maria slowly approached the assistant who had called her.

THE BOTTLE OF MILK

8

The citizens' respect for these workers was similar to that they held for police officers or judges. After all, if the assistants became annoyed with anyone, they could give them less food.

Or spoiled food.

Or even pretend that an item was sold out.

Any protests would only make things worse.

"Bread and milk, please," said Maria.

The assistant was a middle-aged man with sleepy eyes. He turned his back on her and went inside the store.

He returned with two loaves of bread but no milk. Maria gave him a pleading look. She hoped he would offer an explanation.

He didn't.

THE BOTTLE OF MILK

9

"The milk, the milk's missing," Maria murmured.

The assistant bit his lip and sighed. "There's no milk."

"How come there's no milk? Just two days ago there was."

"Sabotage. The enemy is intentionally making things break down. They have managed to sabotage the agricultural production. Didn't you know?" He raised his voice as he asked.

Maria lowered her gaze and swallowed. "Yes, I knew, of course I did..."

"Then why did you ask? Are you trying to say that the Communist Party is incompetent? That they are unable to keep the country running?"

"No, not at all. Sorry."

"Next!" shouted the assistant.

Maria grabbed her loaves, shoved them in her bag, and left. As she passed the line, tears ran down her face.

A few people looked as if they felt sorry for her. Some stared at her with disgust at her tears.

Most ignored her.

10

Maria began her journey home. The sun was starting to warm the city, but it didn't warm her body.

Her feet were frozen, and her steps dragged. Her boots scraped the cement of the pavement as if they were brakes instead of shoes.

The other pedestrians moved fast and ended up bumping into her. She was nothing but a nuisance, an annoyance they wanted out of their way.

One or two people cursed or insulted her. Maria did not even see them or hear them.

Her eyes registered the crowd around her. She saw the buildings and the cars in the streets.

Her nose smelled the bodies of the people

around her and the factories that were running.

She heard the noises of the city. She even heard the insults.

But none of it mattered. She was used to all of it. Had lived her life ignoring it.

What mattered was how to explain to Lia that she had not brought the promised milk.

11

It would not be the first time that she came home nearly empty-handed. Lia was used to disappointment.

She had already begun to understand what sort of society she lived in. She did not even complain.

Still, every time Maria came home empty handed, it tore Maria apart.

Now, she was trying to put herself back together again. She needed to think clearly.

THE BOTTLE OF MILK

12

The problem was the more she thought about it, the worse she felt. She had so few options and didn't like any of them.

She could steal.

She could prostitute herself, selling her body for money.

Or she could become the lover of a Party official so he would buy her food and nice things.

The thought of any of them made her want to vomit.

Even so, for the sake of Lia, maybe she had no other choices.

Plenty of other respectable women had done

it. One friend who understood the new realities of survival told her it was only hard the first time.

Then you got used to it. Like any other routine.

And if you were lucky and the man was kind, sometimes you might even enjoy it.

Maria leant against a wall, opened her mouth, and vomited what little there was.

13

When she got home, she found Lia at the kitchen table, doing her homework. She had eaten a crust of bread from the previous day and drunk a cup of tea.

Lia raised her head, As soon as she saw her mother's face, she knew. As usual, she tried to make Maria feel better.

Save her from the pain. From the embarrassment.

"Never mind, Mum, today I don't even feel like drinking milk."

Maria tried to smile but her lips would not obey. Instead, they twisted. Then her breathing turned to sobs.

At last tears fell. Lia got up and hugged her.

"Don't cry, Mum. It's not your fault. The enemy is

destroying our economy. They want to delay the revolution.

"We were just talking about that in school yesterday. Our teacher said we must be prepared to make sacrifices. But victory is certain."

14

Maria stopped crying, pulled away, and looked at her daughter. Would she ever be able to speak to Lia without fear?

Would she ever be able to tell her what was going on without exposing her to danger?

She had told Lia that her father had been sent by the Party to do important work in another city. They didn't know when he would be back.

But she didn't think Lia believed it.

Had she been taught about that in school? About her father and where he really was?

Would they have mentioned it at all?

She was thinking about this when she heard a

knock on the door.

It's the old man from the grocery line who's come to arrest me.

15

He must have heard her complaints about the milk and told the police.

They had probably been following her for some time. Had probably just been waiting for a single mistake.

Anything that would let them send her to a re-education camp. So many public projects were happening. They needed laborers to finish the work.

And what about Lia? What would happen to her if they took Maria?

No doubt, they would put her in an orphanage. She would suffer ever more hunger and abuse.

Maria had heard rumors of girls being forced to

prostitute themselves with foreign diplomats or lead-
ers of the people.

Worse still, some had preferred suicide.

Maria looked everywhere quickly, as if there
might be a secret passage in her kitchen so they
could escape. For some hideaway where they might
be safe. A magical place where they could live. But
there wasn't one. There never had been.

16

The blows on the door got harder.

The person knocking was getting impatient.

Maria resigned herself to her fate. There was no escaping this and she accepted it.

She would go wherever they sent her.

Do whatever they ordered her to do. Confess whatever they wanted her to say.

She would even swear eternal love for the Party.

Anything to make it easier on Lia.

If criminals behaved well, the Party treated their children better. At least that's what she had heard.

Some even finished their university studies and became Party officials.

Maybe Lia would escape unharmed. She was so brave and strong. She hugged her daughter once more.

Then, like a person heading for execution without fear, she headed to the door.

17

The knocking was softer now. She didn't dare take comfort in that. She knew the games they played to confuse their victims. To give them the hope that they were safe.

It made prison that much more painful. Being given that hope at the very end.

Before she opened the door, she glanced at one of her husband's paintings.

It was a street scene painted in bright colors. Two women and a child in a hat.

It might be the last time she would see it. She remembered him painting it and smiled.

Only then did she raise her hand to the door handle.

Her mouth hung open in shock. She wanted to speak, but she could not say a word.

18

Ruth said nothing either. It was as if there were no words to fit the situation. Even Ruth's eyes were blank.

Then she raised her right arm, handed over the shopping bag, and turned her back.

Maria stood and watched her leave. Her steps beat down the snow.

Only when her neighbor had turned the corner was Maria able to look into the bag.

Her eyes widened. Her hands shook, Laughter and tears came at the same time.

Inside the bag was a bottle of milk.

Tuk-Tuk

Hagai Perets

1

Noise. Chaos. Smells. Trash. People, and people, and people, and more people. Colors.

Everything's overcrowded, packed with people, a total chaotic mess. Cars' exhaust, smoke, and car horns. Cows, and the smell of manure left behind. And people, and more people.

What are we doing here?

We're packed in a tiny tuk-tuk, zig-zagging in a sea of people, cars, trucks, and every possible type of vehicle on wheels. Small kids cling to the windshield, pushing their small hands through the half-opened window. They beg, "Please, sir, please."

The street vendors, the smell, and the people, so many people. How can the tuk-tuk even pass through? Every other second I choke a scream as it almost runs over a pedestrian, hits a biker, or crashes into a truck. But every time, in the last moment possible, it just sharply turns.

At the same time, it reminds me of a water stream. It smoothly flows around rocks in these endless human currents. No thoughts, no plans, just flow. I wish I could flow like this, with no thoughts, just alive and moving.

Noah and Jill are closely packed between us. Rachel looks through the window, somehow unbothered by the trash everywhere and the kids' hands pushing through the window. Or maybe not.

I don't know how to read her anymore. Once, I thought I knew what she was thinking just by a look. Now, I'm not sure I ever understood her.

What are we doing here? Why did I think anything would be different here, that here we'd have another chance to fix everything?

With another sharp move of the tuk-tuk squeezing me into the window, one of the bags almost falls on me. The bags are all pressed behind us. I'm counting. One, two, three, four, five. And "our life" —that's what we started calling the passports and money pouch that now seems to be welded to my skin—six.

Through the airport transfers, the trains, buses, and taxis, I got used to counting. Every time I have my eye on the bags, I count. One, two, three, four, five, "our life"—six.

Everything is here. Everything's OK. Like a mantra, holding me. But that's it; we're almost there. Just one more left turn at the end of the world, almost ready to begin our real journey.

2

I take a quick look at Rachel, who's packed between the bags and the kids. I try to guess what she thinks, and what she thinks of me now, and of this place. How have I managed to persuade her to leave everything and go on this crazy trip?

I remember an old Hasidic saying: Wherever you go, you'll find something to fix there. I can't even remember the exact phrase now, but there's so much that needs fixing. How do I even begin? And what does it matter now?

Wherever I go, I always carry myself with me. Why would this trip help or change anything? But maybe... Maybe this is our chance to go back to our old selves, to the burning passion we used to feel.

We just need to get out of this craziness and we'll get there. We'll find peace. Just us, and the kids, and the quiet people told us about.

A deafening horn and another sharp turn wake me back to reality. Another wiggle and the tuk-tuk stops.

"Here you are, sir," the driver says, turning toward me. "Twenty rupees, please."

I try to take the wallet out of "our life," but between the kids and the bags, I can hardly move. It's stuck behind my back. I'm already sweating, and the smells here just drive me crazy. I undo the belt strap and pull it until the pouch is out. I search inside and take out the wallet, trying to see which bill is twenty rupees.

"Thank you, sir," the driver says. He turns back, waiting for us to get off the tuk-tuk.

I start pulling and pushing the bags, one after the other, while Rachel and the kids get out through the other door. I try to watch the bags I've put on the pavement, and at the same time watch over Rachel and the kids. They seem to be almost swept away by the currents of people and vehicles before they reach the safe shore on the other side of the street.

The last one out is the kids' toy bag. I close the door. The driver, not even looking back, drives away and disappears through the traffic.

3

That's it. We stand by a small mountain of bags. An island of stillness between the waves of people. Two adults and two kids.

Jill holds my hand, and Noah holds Rachel's hand. They look so lost right now, while the people-currents flow around our little island. The noise starts closing over me. I look for a quieter place.

"Let's go to the fruit stand over there," I say, pointing.

Rachel and I take the bags in our hands and we all find a way through, somehow. At last, a quieter place where we can get organized.

The bags are piled up again. I count. One, two, three, four, five, and "our life"—I put my hands on my hips. But it's not there.

In all the moving around and carrying the bags, I haven't noticed the constant pressure on my hips is gone. I forgot I untied the straps to pay the driver.

I dig through the pile of bags. It probably just fell between them. I move them around, but it's not there.

"Jake? Is everything OK?" Rachel asks.

"Yes, sure," I lie.

It feels like my chest is tightening. Panic.

The pouch, "our life," was left on the tuk-tuk seat.

I turn back, looking at the street. The raging river of people and vehicles is still there. I can't even see where we got out of the tuk-tuk.

Maybe it fell on the way from the tuk-tuk? I try to retrace our path from the street in my mind.

The money, the passports, the maps... everything's in there. Rachel told me it's better not to put all our eggs in one basket, but I wanted to be sure that everything was on me, all the time. I even slept with the pouch on me.

What do I do now? My body feels burning all over. I wipe sweat from my forehead. What do we do now?

We need to call someone. Talk with the embassy. But where would we find a public phone? We have no idea of their number. We can't even pay for a place to sleep. We don't even have the money to pay for a phone call. We have nothing!

Rachel will surely kill me now. She already thinks I'm irresponsible, and that it was crazy to take this trip to begin with. It took me months to persuade her. And now? Nothing.

We have nothing. There's no way Rachel will give us another chance now.

With all the flights and buses, and the feeling that everything here stinks, it's ugly. The words between us have just become harsher and harsher until we've stopped talking at all, besides what we have to for the kids.

I try to keep my voice normal. "I'll go over and get us something to eat," I say.

Rachel looks at me with a questioning look. Food? Now? I read on her face.

I turn and go before she'll have time to ask me.

4

I squeeze myself through the people again, pushing through.

Where did we get off the tuk-tuk, exactly?

I look right and left. I stop for a second and almost get run over by a bike coming from the other side. I keep on moving. Then I see the colored pavement where we got off, I think. I keep on pushing through until I get there.

What now?

It's so hot, I take off my sweatshirt. Somehow, even with all of this noise, I can hear my heart beating: tuk – tuk – tuk. Or maybe I'm imagining this?

I turn around everywhere, looking for our tuk-

tuk, but I know it's hopeless. It disappeared a moment after we got off. I'm trying to find one tuk-tuk in a city of millions and total chaos. I have no idea who the driver is or how to find him.

The pressure in my stomach and chest keeps growing. The heartbeats, and the heat, and this horrible smell and noise—I have to breathe. I have to get out from all of these people. I have to sit down and just breathe. Something is wrong with my breathing.

I turn around to look, and turn again. People are everywhere, surrounding me, pushing me, crowding me. They're moving, sweating, noisy. Then I think I see our tuk-tuk on the other side of the street.

I start pushing through. I lose it for a moment, and then find it again. Another push, but then I realize. It's not him.

Fantasies, illusions... How long will I fool myself?

Now I'm just trying to waste time before I'll have to go back to Rachel and tell her. The last grains of sand are falling through the hourglass of our marriage. What will happen to Noah and Jill?

I try to wait one more moment, looking around. One last turn.

Nothing.

What will we do tonight? Surely we'll find someone to let us make a phone call. But who should we call? And how would that help us? It's like the whole world comes crashing down on me. I can't even move anymore. I'm paralyzed. And the heat—it's burning! I feel nausea and everything seems to spin around me. Rachel will never forgive me...

Then something touches my shoulder.

"Sir? Sir?"

I turn around.

"Here you are, sir."

It's our tuk-tuk driver, handing me "our life" through the window.

"Have a good day, sir."

I don't even get a chance to answer. He drives away again into the chaos.

I'm standing, still shocked. "Our life" is in my hand. "Our life" returned to us.

Everything is OK now.

Twenty years later, it's still one of the happiest moments in my life.

988

Phoebe Angaye

1

With each 988 call, I swear I get more swole.

Right now, the person beneath me is trying to shimmy up and down ike a pig taking a roll in the mud. With all the tossing and turning, they might slip out of my chain-linked arms like butter. Good thing I have my needle.

With a click, the piercing sting of my hair-thin needle slips in between the folds of the man's skin. Slowly, his tomato-red face begins to drain out to his normal color. For a 50-year-old man, this dude can kick some butt. He flops over my shoulder as his eyelids begin to droop.

Another person saved.

"There, there. We'll get you taken care of, okay?" I say, as the paramedics take him off me and place him on the stretcher.

"Nice job as always, Winston."

Ah, I'd know that sarcastic southern drawl anywhere. I turn to see my partner, the officer, Stephan Barry.

You could practically mistake his head for a bowling ball with how shiny it is. I think it's stress that took his hair, not the fact he's in his forties. And of course, give him some donuts and he could be the mascot for police officers everywhere.

Well, police officers may need one with the way people are trashing them. In fact, I can feel the "friendliest" gaze from the family I just helped directed at Stephan. He notices, but doesn't care.

I chuckle. "All in a day's work."

The ambulance flashes its light like it's trying to send Morse code to us as it drives away down the street. The family comes towards me with hugs and words of kindness, but not for Stephan. I can't say I don't understand, with all the controversy surrounding police officers at the moment.

That's where we come in. Mental health officers.

We're trained to deescalate, and not use deadly force. Call 988, and we'll be on the way. We're trained in psychology and we seek the best solution for each person we help. Not to dunk on police officers, but we have next to zero deaths compared to police officers. And the people we help have a higher chance of coming out alive, which is a bonus, too.

In light of all the controversies, it's no wonder mental health officers were created as a profession. And that's where I come in.

I'm the yin to Stephan's yang. All mental health officers are the yin to police officers' yang. If things get too difficult or violent, the police officer can use lethal force. Of course, we never let it get to that.

Once the family has finished showering me with praise, Stephan and I go back to the car. I can see from the corner of my eye how Stephan has practically chained his jaw shut.

I sigh. Okay. Turning my therapist mode on.

"You don't have to be upset at the family for ignoring you. It's just with all the incidents involving police—" I start to say.

Stephan lets out a snort. "That kind of mentality is stupid," he says. "A society will always need law and order. Society will always need someone to enforce the law. Police officers aren't going anywhere."

Oh, goodie. Here we go again.

"Yes, society needs someone to enforce the law," I say. "But maybe the way police officers went about enforcing the law created this antagonism—"

I nearly fly out of my seat as Stephan brakes. I

swear my heart nearly flew out of my chest, too. I glare at Stephan from the side of my eye. He's cool as a cucumber.

"You need to understand, kid. There are just some people who will not be helped by anyone. And you need to recognize that," Stephan mutters, driving once the light turns green.

I keep my mouth shut because I know this conversation will just go around in circles if I let it.

I'm not a kid. I'm twenty years old. And I know, deep in my soul, everyone has something in them that can be helped. We were all born without judgement. Who are we to say who can and cannot be saved?

2

"Please come to this address, we need help, qui—"

The voice fizzes out like a shaken soda. We just finished our rounds at this house, and now a distress call?

Stephan plugs in the coordinates of the address. I look it up. A café? That's a new one.

Stephan practically does a fast marathon, enough to challenge Usain Bolt for his title. In a matter of seconds, we're already there. Stephan has his gun holstered, and I have mine. Not that I need it, it's just for show for me. Mental health officers rarely use our guns.

Stephan and I open the door and step in. I try to keep a poker face, but I can't.

Dozens of men and women sit beneath their tables, trembling like leaves in the wind. In the middle of the café is a man. He's scrawny, like a starving rat craving for flesh. His beard takes up half of his face, allowing us to only make out his mouth.

In his hand? A gun.

He snarls when he sees us. Stephan puts his hand on his holster, but I smack it away. I shake my head at him. That could just anger the man. I turn back to the shooter with the friendliest smile I can muster.

"Hey. We're here to help, okay? We're here to listen," I say. "My name is Winston and this is my partner, Stephan. We're not going to hurt you. We just want to make sure you and everyone here are safe. What's your name?"

I keep a level tone. He needs to be comfortable with us in order for him to trust us. The man gives a hearty chuckle and swings his gun in an infinity symbol around the room. Stephan tenses. My heart nearly shatters on the floor.

"Joey. But why does it matter? We're all going to die here together! We're all going down!" he hisses through his teeth.

I inch closer. Joey tenses.

"We don't have to die together. We can all leave together. Safe and sound. I know this isn't you," I tell him. "I know you want people to recognize your pain. I do. I see your pain, and I can see you're hurting. Let the other people go and take me, okay?" My voice wobbles in the middle.

I can't mess this up. So many lives are on the line. Stephan is ready to shoot the guy dead, but I can't let him. I know this guy can be saved. I know he can come back from this. I've seen so many people make a comeback. I know he's one of them.

I look him in the eye. "Please, Joey. Please let them go."

Joey holds my gaze for a moment. Then looks down at the floor. And then—

BAM! BAM! BAM!

The world seems to go into slow motion. Three bullets ricochet into civilians' backs as they scream. Some bodies instantly turn lifeless.

All the color is sucked from my vision. In the next moments, I'm not in control. Someone else is. My hand grabs my gun from its holster and—

BAM! BAM! BAM!

Three tiny little bullets hit Joey. The gun flies out of his hand and smashes down on the floor.

I did that. I just killed someone.

The rest of the civilians get up and they're cheering. But I can't say the same for myself. I took a life that had promise. That could have been better. Someone squeezes my shoulder.

Stephan. He purses his lips before speaking.

"I know this is hard. But sometimes in life, no matter what you do, blood will be shed. That's life, kid. No matter what choice you make, even the right ones."

I can't talk back. My voice is trapped inside my throat, a prisoner.

But when I look forward, I see a jarring light poking at my eyes. The cloak of darkness over me has now been lifted, bringing me out of the cave that trapped me.

Now, I can see. But the light feels like blazing fires, and now I know I can never go back.

About the Authors

João Cerqueira is the author of nine books and is published in eight countries: Portugal, Spain, Italy, France, England, United States, Brazil, and Argentina. He won the 2020 Indie Reader Awards, the 2014 Global ebook Awards and the 2013 USA Best Book Awards. An excerpt of the novel *Perestroika*—"The Bottle of Milk"—was published by Storyshares.

Hagai Perets and Phoebe Angaye are contributing authors to the Storyshares library.

About the Publisher

Storyshares is a publisher focused on supporting the millions of teens and adults who struggle with reading by creating a new shelf in the library specifically for them. The ever-growing collection features content that is compelling and culturally relevant for teens and adults, yet still readable at a range of lower reading levels.

Storyshares generates content by engaging deeply with writers, bringing together a community to create this new kind of book. With more intriguing and approachable stories to choose from, the teens and adults who have fallen behind are improving their skills and beginning to discover the joy of reading.

For more information, visit storyshares.org.

Easy to Read. Hard to Put Down.